Do Legendary Shit

Your Personal Money Playbook

Advik Dhand

Dedication

To every young dreamer who believes money is more than numbers on a page this book is for you. May it give you the tools, courage, and vision to build the life you imagine.

To my dad, whose background in finance and constant encouragement inspired me to think beyond school routines and discover the practical side of life. Your wisdom and example planted the seed for this book, and your influence continues to guide me on this journey.

And to my family, who taught me the value of patience, perseverance, and curiosity—your love is the foundation on which this book stands.

Acknowledgment

This book would not have been possible without the support and inspiration of many people.

First, to my dad your background in finance and encouragement to think beyond school routines inspired the very ideas in these pages. To my parents, thank you for teaching me discipline, curiosity, and the values that matter most.

This project also grew out of my TEDx journey. While preparing my talk on finance, I realized I had far more to share than a single speech could hold. That summer, I began writing, and this book came to life.

I am also grateful to the works of Robert Kiyosaki, whose lessons continue to inspire me.

Most of all, thank you to the readers. If these words help you see money in a new way, then my purpose has been fulfilled.

About the Author

Advik Dhand is a young author and speaker deeply passionate about financial education and helping young people understand money in a practical way. Inspired by his dad's background in finance, Advik always questioned the "school-only" way of learning, seeking real-life lessons and stories.

Before writing *Do Legendary Shit: Your Personal Money Playbook*, Advik wrote two books which are available online, where he began exploring ideas, experimenting with storytelling, and building his voice. These earlier works gave him the confidence and experience needed to take on bigger projects. While the focus of his new book is finance, those earlier books helped him learn discipline in writing, how to connect with readers, and the joy of sharing knowledge.

When not writing or speaking, Advik loves to play guitar, explore new ideas, solve problems, and find practical ways to apply financial concepts in everyday life. His goal is simple: to empower young readers to take control of their financial future and believe that they can make a difference starting now.

Table of Contents

Dedication i

Acknowledgment ii

About the Author iii

Introduction 1

Chapter 1: The Language of Money 7

Chapter 2: Earn First, Then Learn 13

Chapter 3: Spend Smart, Not Fast 19

Chapter 4: Balance Sheet 24

Chapter 5: The Income and Expense Statement 30

Chapter 6: Cash Flow Statement 38

Chapter 7: Assets Make You Rich 43

Chapter 8: Your First Financial Goal 49

Chapter 9: Be the CEO of You Inc 57

Chapter 10: What Are Stocks 64

Chapter 11: What Is Real Estate 70

Chapter 12: Risk and Reward 76

Chapter 13: Start Your Own Business 83

Chapter 14: Compound Growth — Your Money's Superpower 92

Your Money Playbook: One Last Pass 100

Introduction

Have you ever heard someone say, *"Money doesn't grow on trees"*? Adults love using that phrase, especially when kids ask for something that costs money. But have you ever paused to think about what it really means? If money doesn't grow on trees, then where does it come from?

The answer is simple but powerful: money comes from solving problems.

It doesn't appear through luck, wishing, or hoping someone hands it to you. It shows up when a person creates value for someone else. That could mean cooking a meal, building a house, designing a toy, fixing a sink, or even inventing a brand-new app that millions of people enjoy. Every time money changes hands, there's value at the center.

That's the first big lesson of this book. When you understand that money is tied to value, you stop seeing it as mysterious or magical. Instead, you see it as something that flows — from the person who needs something to the person who can provide it.

Think about it. If you babysit for your neighbor, they're paying you because they value their child's safety and your time. If your parents order pizza, they're paying because they value a hot meal prepared by someone else. If someone buys a video game, they're paying for fun and entertainment. The situations may change, but money always follows value.

Here's the exciting part: you can create value at any age. Kids are just as capable of solving problems as adults, even if the problems are smaller or simpler. That's why this book isn't about waiting until you're older to learn about money.

It's about starting now, so you can use these lessons for the rest of your life.

So let's begin with the most important question: how does money actually move?

The Two Main Types of Income

When you look closely at the money world, you'll find there are two main ways people earn:

- Earned income
- Passive income

They may sound simple, but these two categories are the foundation for everything else you'll learn.

Earned Income: Trading Time for Dollars

Earned income is money you receive by directly working. You show up, complete a task, put in the time — and then you get paid. This is the kind of income most people know best.

For example:

- You mow your neighbor's lawn for ten dollars.
- You babysit for a few hours and earn fifteen dollars.
- You set up a lemonade stand on a hot day and make a few quarters at a time.
- An adult clocks in at their job and earns a salary or hourly wage.

The trade is always the same: you give your time and energy, and in return you get money.

The best part of earned income is that it's fast and predictable. If you work today, you'll usually get paid today or soon after. For kids, it's a fantastic way to learn responsibility, discipline, and the connection between effort and reward.

But here's the catch: you only have so many hours in a day. If you stop working, the money stops too. That's why earned income, while valuable, has limits. You can't trade time forever — which is where the second type of income comes in.

Passive Income: Money That Works for You

Passive income is different. Instead of working for every dollar, you build or invest in something that keeps earning even when you're not actively working. Some people call this *"making money while you sleep."* It might sound magical, but it's really the result of smart systems or investments.

Examples of passive income include:

- You design stickers or a coloring book, post them online, and earn money every time someone buys one.
- You invest twenty dollars in a company's stock, and over time, you receive dividends.
- You place a gumball machine in a store and refill it once a week, but it earns quarters all week long.
- You write a comic book once, but each new sale brings in more money.

The difference is simple: earned income means you work for money, while passive income means money works for you.

Neither one is better or worse. Both matter. But the real power comes when you combine them — working to earn money, then using some of it to build systems or assets that keep paying you long after the work is done.

The Story of Elijah: The Ten Dollar Lawn vs. the Two Dollar Comic

Elijah was a kid who wanted to earn money during summer break. One day, he mowed his neighbor's lawn for ten dollars. It took an hour of hard work under the hot sun, and when he finished, he felt proud. The ten dollars went straight into his savings jar. That was earned income.

The next week, Elijah tried something new. He had drawn a funny comic book about a superhero dog. He spent two dollars making copies and shared them with friends and family. They loved it. His cousin posted it online, and soon Elijah had sold ten copies for twenty dollars.

Here's the key difference: mowing the lawn earned him ten dollars for one hour of work. But the comic kept making money even after he'd finished drawing it. That was the beginning of passive income.

Elijah realized something important: lawn money was good, but limited to how many lawns he could mow. The comic, however, could be sold again and again with almost no extra work.

That lesson stuck with him: when you build something once that keeps paying later, you're not just earning — you're building freedom.

Why This Matters for You

When you're young, most of your money will come from earned income — chores, babysitting, mowing lawns, allowance. That's normal and good. It teaches you to value work and understand how money flows.

But even now, you can start asking bigger questions:

- What can I create once that keeps earning again and again?
- What can I invest in that doesn't depend only on my time?

Thinking this way builds a new kind of money mindset. Many people grow up believing the only way to earn more is to work harder or longer. But that's not true. The secret lies in combining earned and passive income, so your effort today can create rewards tomorrow.

Start Small, Think Big

You don't need a big business or a lot of money to begin building passive income. All you need is creativity, effort, and the right mindset. Even something small — like crafts, stories, or digital products — can grow into a system that pays over and over again.

What you need is:

- A skill or talent (drawing, baking, coding, building, storytelling)
- A way to turn that skill into something valuable
- A way to share or sell it more than once

The earlier you begin, the stronger your results. Imagine planting a tiny tree in your backyard. At first, it doesn't look like much. But if you water it, protect it, and let it grow, one day it provides shade, fruit, and a place to rest. Passive income works the same way — start small, and with time and care, it grows into something powerful.

What You've Learned

1. Money doesn't just appear — it flows from solving problems and creating value.
2. Earned income comes from trading your time and effort for money.
3. Passive income comes from building or investing in something that keeps paying you.
4. You don't need to wait until you're older to start thinking about both.

In the next chapter, we'll explore spending — and how to keep your money strong instead of watching it disappear the moment it arrives. Because earning is only the first step; spending wisely is what keeps your money growing.

Chapter 1:
The Language of Money

If you've ever traveled to a country where you didn't speak the language, you know how confusing it can be. People may be talking all around you, yet you can't quite follow what's being said. Maybe you're in a restaurant, trying to order food, but the menu is in another language — and you're not sure if you just asked for chicken soup or octopus salad.

Money works the same way. It has its own language, and if you don't understand it, you can get lost. The problem is that most people live in a world full of money without ever learning its language. They know how to spend it, and maybe even how to earn it, but not how it works, grows, and flows.

Robert Kiyosaki, in *Rich Dad Poor Dad*, once wrote: *"Money comes and goes, but if you have the education about how money works, you gain power over it and can begin building wealth."* Think of that as learning the grammar, vocabulary, and pronunciation of money. Without these tools, you'll always need a "translator" — someone else making financial decisions for you — and that can be risky.

Why We Call It a Language

Languages have words, rules, and meaning. The language of money is no different. It has words like income, expenses, profit, debt, interest, and assets. It has rules — such as how taxes work, how to calculate value, and how supply and demand affect prices. And it has meaning — the most important part, because without meaning, the words are just noise.

Imagine two kids looking at the same $10 bill. One sees "candy, toys, and fun." The other sees "a chance to invest and grow more money." The bill hasn't changed, but their understanding of it — their *language skills* — is completely different.

The second kid isn't necessarily smarter, but they've learned the words and concepts of money in a way that shapes how they use it. That's the power of financial literacy.

The First Words in Your Money Vocabulary

When you start learning any new language, you begin with simple words — hello, goodbye, thank you. In the language of money, those basic words are: earn, spend, save, invest.

- Earn means to receive money in exchange for your time, skills, or ideas.
- Spend means to use money to get something you want or need.
- Save means to keep some of your money for later instead of spending it all.
- Invest means to use your money in a way that helps it grow over time.

If you only know "earn" and "spend," you'll never build lasting wealth. That's like learning a few words in Spanish but not enough to hold a conversation. You'll be stuck asking, *"Where is the bathroom?"* for the rest of your life.

A Story from the Playground

I knew a boy named Leo who loved trading cards. At recess, kids would gather in circles and swap cards — one for one, or sometimes two for one if the card was rare.

One day, Leo traded one of his cards for a chocolate bar. It was delicious, but gone in a few minutes. Another kid, Sarah, traded her card for three others she knew were more valuable in the long run. She didn't get the instant joy of chocolate, but later she traded those three cards for a super-rare one worth much more than anything else in the group.

Leo spent. Sarah invested.

Without realizing it, Sarah was speaking the language of money — she understood value, trade, and delayed gratification. Leo was still learning his first few "words."

Why Adults Struggle With the Language

You'd think that once people grow up, they'd be fluent in the language of money. But many adults are like tourists who've lived in a foreign country for years without ever learning the language. They get by, but they never master it.

Robert Kiyosaki tells a story about how his "poor dad" — a well-educated man — believed that getting a good job and working hard was the path to financial success. But he never really learned the language of money, so he spent everything he earned. His "rich dad" had less formal education, but he understood how money worked. He learned about assets, investments, and cash flow — and that fluency made him wealthy.

The lesson? It's not how much money you make. It's how well you speak its language.

Grammar and Rules of Money

In English, we follow certain rules: subjects come before verbs, and sentences end with punctuation. In money, the rules are different but just as important:

- You can't spend more than you earn without creating debt.
- If you invest money, it can grow through compound interest.
- If you let inflation eat away at your savings, your money loses value.

Understanding these rules is like knowing when to use "their" versus "there." Get it wrong, and the meaning changes completely — except in money, the consequences are bigger than just a spelling mistake.

Becoming Fluent

Learning to speak the language of money isn't something you master in a day. It's a skill you develop over time by listening, practicing, and making mistakes.

You can read books, watch videos, and ask questions. But the best way to learn is by using it in real life — earning, saving, investing, and tracking what happens. Every financial decision is practice.

And just like learning a spoken language, the earlier you start, the easier it becomes. Kids who learn about money early gain an advantage. They grow up making smarter decisions, avoiding common traps, and building a foundation that supports them for life.

A Small Exercise

Look at the money you have right now — whether it's coins in a jar, a few bills in your wallet, or numbers on a bank app. Ask yourself:

- Where did it come from? (earn)
- What do I plan to do with it? (spend, save, invest)
- Will it grow or shrink over time?

This little habit trains your brain to think in the language of money. Over time, you'll start noticing opportunities and risks you once missed.

Why This Matters

Speaking the language of money isn't about becoming greedy. It's about freedom. It's about having choices. When you're fluent, you can decide where to live, what to do, and how to spend your time — instead of letting money decide for you.

As Robert Kiyosaki said: *"The single most powerful asset we all have is our mind. If it is trained well, it can create enormous wealth."* Learning the language of money is training your mind.

And the best part? Once you learn it, no one can take it away from you.

Key Points

- Money is a tool for exchange.
- We work, earn money, and solve problems.
- Knowing how to use money gives you the power to build.
- Example: Lemonade stand.
- Example 2: A builder uses tools. You use money.
- Visual: Infographic showing a shovel for gardening, a paintbrush for art, and money for freedom.

Chapter 2:
Earn First, Then Learn

Have you ever heard the phrase *"money doesn't grow on trees"*? Adults love saying that. But if money doesn't grow on trees, where does it actually come from?

The answer might surprise you: *money comes from solving problems.*

- Not from being lucky.
- Not from wishing.
- And definitely not from doing nothing.

Here's why: when people earn money, it's almost always because they created some form of value for someone else. A cook prepares a meal that satisfies hunger. A mechanic fixes a car so it runs again. A tutor helps someone understand a subject they were struggling with. A designer creates a product that makes everyday life easier.

In each of these cases, money isn't random—it's the direct result of exchanging effort, skill, or creativity for something another person needs. That's how the flow of money connects to the flow of value.

The truth is, every dollar someone earns is tied to this exchange. Whether you're a kid earning allowance for chores or an adult working a full-time job, money moves toward the people providing solutions, services, or resources that matter.

So how do you start earning? And more importantly— how do you earn in ways that build over time?

In the world of money, there are two main categories of income:

1. Earned Income – money made directly by working, usually trading time, skill, or labor.
2. Passive Income – money generated from assets, investments, or systems that continue producing value without constant effort.

Let's take a closer look at both.

Earned Income: Trading Time for Dollars:

Earned income is the money you receive when you actively do something—like working, selling, or performing a task.

This is the kind of income most people recognize because it's the foundation of nearly every paycheck and wage system.

For example:

- You mow your neighbor's lawn for 10 dollars.
- You walk a dog for 5 dollars.
- You run a lemonade stand and sell drinks all afternoon.
- Adults go to jobs and get paid hourly wages or a fixed salary.

In all of these cases, you're trading your time, energy, and skills for money. You must show up and complete the work in order to get paid.

Earned income is useful because it teaches responsibility, discipline, and consistency. It also produces immediate results—you put in work today, and the money is in your hand today.

But there's a limitation: you can only work a certain number of hours in a day. If you stop working, the money flow stops too. Time becomes the ceiling on how much you can earn.

And that's where passive income enters the picture.

Passive Income: Money That Works for You:

Passive income is money that comes in without requiring you to be actively present every time it's earned.

It may sound like magic, but it's actually built on systems, ownership, or investments that continue producing value after the initial setup.

Examples of passive income:

1. You write and sell a comic book. Each time someone buys it online, you get a royalty—even while you're asleep.
2. You invest 20 dollars in a company's stock. If the company grows, it sends you 1 dollar in dividends every few months.
3. You design stickers or t-shirts and upload them to a website. Once they're listed, the site handles orders, payments, and shipping.

4. You build a gumball machine and place it in a store. It earns quarters every day, and you only need to restock it weekly.

The difference is structural:

- Earned income = you work for money.
- Passive income = money works for you.

Both types are valuable, but they function in very different ways.

The 10 Dollar Mow vs. The 2 Dollar Comic

Let's look at an example that shows the contrast clearly.

Meet Elijah. One summer, Elijah made 10 dollars mowing his neighbor's lawn. It took him about an hour. He was proud of his effort, and the 10 dollars went straight into his savings jar.

The next week, Elijah used 2 dollars to print and sell a comic book he had drawn. His friends and family loved it, and his cousin posted it online. Within a few days, Elijah sold ten copies and made back 20 dollars total.

Here's the difference:

- The 10 dollars from mowing was *earned income.* Elijah worked for it directly.
- The 20 dollars from comics included *passive income.* Once the comic was created, the money kept coming in—even when he wasn't actively selling.

Elijah still had to mow lawns if he wanted another 10 dollars. But the comic could be sold repeatedly with very little extra work.

That's how passive income scales beyond time.

Why This Matters:

When you're young, most of your money will come from earned income—chores, small jobs, or allowance. That's normal and valuable because it helps you build habits and understand the effort behind each dollar.

But there's also the bigger question: What can you create once that continues to generate money in the future?

This is the difference between money tasks (work that stops when you stop) and money systems (work that continues producing results after it's set up).

Start Small. Think Big:

Creating passive income doesn't require being rich or even being an adult.

You only need:

- A skill or talent (drawing, writing, coding, baking, organizing).
- A way to package that skill into something valuable.
- A plan to share, sell, or distribute it more than once.

Even simple projects—like a coloring book, digital stories, sticker designs, or craft tutorials online—can create small but steady streams of passive income.

What You've Learned

- Money can come from more than just showing up to work.
- *Earned income* provides fast results and builds responsibility.
- Passive income requires creativity and planning but creates ongoing rewards.
- Even small ideas can grow into money systems.

Key Points:

- How people (including kids) make money.
- Two types of income: earned (jobs, chores, business) and passive (interest, royalties, investments).
- Not all money works in the same way.
- Example: 10 dollars from mowing vs. a 2-dollar comic that keeps earning.
- Visual idea: Flowchart showing how earned income stops when work stops, while passive income keeps flowing once created.

Chapter 3:
Spend Smart, Not Fast

Have you ever felt that rush of excitement the second you had money in your pocket?

Maybe you walked into a store, saw a cool pair of sneakers or the latest toy, and thought, *"I have to get this right now."* The feeling was so strong it almost felt impossible to wait.

Spending money feels fun. That's no secret.

But here's the big lesson of this chapter: just because you can spend your money doesn't mean you should.

Smart spenders understand something impulsive spenders often overlook: every dollar is a future decision. When you spend it today, you're saying "no" to something you could have had tomorrow.

Let's slow down and explore how to make smart choices instead of fast ones.

Needs vs. Wants

Before spending money, ask one powerful question: *Do I need this, or do I just want it?*

A need is something essential for your well-being, safety, or survival. These include:

- Food
- Clothing

- Shelter
- Transportation
- Basic school supplies

A want is something extra—fun, exciting, or trendy, but not required for living. These include:

- Designer shoes
- Video games
- Fancy snacks
- Latest gadgets

Wants aren't bad. In fact, enjoying wants is part of life. But if you always put wants first, your money may vanish before covering your real needs.

Spending smart begins with recognizing this difference. Once you can separate wants from needs, planning becomes easier.

What Is Delayed Gratification?

Imagine two choices:

1. Spend ten dollars today on a cool t-shirt.
2. Save that same ten dollars every week for two months and buy a brand-new mountain bike.

Most people will say the bike is the smarter choice—but in the moment, waiting feels hard. That's why delayed gratification is one of the most powerful money skills.

Delayed gratification means choosing a bigger reward later instead of a smaller reward right now. It's the ability to wait, and it's a skill that pays off in almost every area of life—money, school, and even friendships.

People who learn this skill tend to save more, make stronger choices, and reach their long-term goals. And like any skill, it can be practiced until it becomes natural.

Story Time: Sneakers vs. Mountain Bike

Meet Jaden.

Jaden had been saving birthday money, weekly allowance, and cash from helping his cousin clean out the garage. After just over a month, he had sixty-five dollars.

That weekend, Jaden went to the mall with his friends. They spotted a pair of bright, limited-edition sneakers in the store window. His friends rushed in to try them on.

"They're so sick," one of them said. "You should get a pair."

Jaden picked up a box. The price tag? Exactly sixty dollars.

He thought about the sneakers, then remembered something else—a mountain bike he'd seen at a sporting goods store. It cost two hundred dollars, and he'd been dreaming about it for weeks.

Jaden had a choice:

Spend nearly all his money now, or wait and keep saving for the bike.

"I'll wait," he finally said, putting the sneakers back.

His friends were surprised. Some teased him. It wasn't easy to say no in that moment.

But two months later, Jaden had saved enough to buy the bike. The first time he rode it down the trail near his neighborhood, wind in his face and speed under his feet, he couldn't stop smiling.

The sneakers would have been fun for a while. But the bike gave him freedom—and that feeling lasted far longer.

The Smart Spending Formula

Here's a simple way to think before you spend:

- Ask: Do I need this, or do I just want it?
- Ask: Will I still care about this a week from now?
- Ask: If I wait, could I afford something even better?
- Decide: Is this the best use of my money right now?

If the answer is "no," pause and wait.

If the answer is "yes," go ahead—but track what you spend.

Every spending choice has a trade-off. Fast spending makes money disappear. Smart spending makes money build.

Saving Makes Spending More Powerful

Saving isn't about saying "no" to fun. It's about saying "yes" to better fun later.

When you save first, you give yourself more freedom and more choices. Even a small habit—like saving five dollars a week—can grow into something meaningful.

And when you finally buy what you've been saving for, the pride feels as good as the purchase. Because you didn't just spend quickly—you spent with purpose.

What You've Learned

You now know:

- The difference between needs and wants.
- That every dollar you spend is also a choice about your future.
- That waiting, even when difficult, can lead to bigger rewards.
- How spending smart is about building something— not just buying something.

In the next chapter, we'll take a closer look at how to measure what you own and what you owe—your personal financial scorecard.

That's where your real money power begins.

Key Points:

Understanding needs versus wants.

- Practicing delayed gratification.
- Every dollar is a future choice.
- Mini-story: Buying sneakers now versus saving for a mountain bike later.
- Visual: A scale showing sneakers vs. bike, and a calendar tracking weekly savings.

Chapter 4:
Balance Sheet

Every athlete has a scoreboard.

It tells them how many points they've scored and whether they're winning or losing the game.

Now imagine if you had a scoreboard for your money—a way to see exactly where you stand. That's what a balance sheet does.

A balance sheet is your personal money scoreboard. It shows what you own, what you owe, and how much you're really worth financially.

And here's the key: it's not just for adults or businesses—you can use it too.

Let's break it down.

What You Own: Assets

The first side of your balance sheet lists your assets.

Assets are anything you own that has value. They can be small or large. If it's something you could sell, trade, or use to create future opportunities, it's usually an asset.

For kids, assets might include:

- Cash in your piggy bank or savings account
- Gift cards with money left on them

- A valuable toy, collectible, or device you could resell
- Money someone owes you (an IOU)
- A small business or side hustle you've started (like mowing lawns or selling crafts)

As you grow older, assets can include things such as:

- Stocks or investments that pay dividends
- A bike or laptop you purchased and still hold value in
- Property or something you could rent out for income
- Intellectual property (like a song you wrote, a design you created, or a digital product online)

Assets are important because they give you financial strength and flexibility. The more assets you build, the more choices and opportunities you create for your future.

What You Owe: Liabilities

The other side of your balance sheet shows your liabilities.

Liabilities are debts—anything you owe that must be paid back. Even kids can have them.

Examples include:

- Borrowing five dollars from your sibling to buy snacks
- Promising to pay back a friend who covered your movie ticket

- Using allowance money early and agreeing to "owe" it back next week

Liabilities aren't automatically bad. Sometimes borrowing helps you get something you need sooner. But if you don't track them carefully, they can quietly pile up and weaken your financial position.

A healthy balance sheet means keeping liabilities small, clear, and manageable.

Net Worth: The Big Picture

Here's the part that ties it all together.

When you subtract your liabilities from your assets, you get your net worth.

This number is the "score" that shows how strong your financial position really is.

The formula is simple:

Net Worth = Assets – Liabilities

Example:

- You have fifty dollars in your savings jar.
- Your cousin owes you ten dollars (an IOU).
- But you also owe five dollars to your older brother.

Assets = $50 + $10 = $60
Liabilities = $5
Net Worth = $60 – $5 = $55

Your net worth = fifty-five dollars.

This number can rise or fall.

- Saving more, earning more, or getting repaid makes your assets grow.
- Borrowing too much or not paying people back makes your liabilities grow.

By tracking your net worth, you start thinking differently: *"Will this choice grow or shrink my balance sheet?"*

Why It Matters

You might wonder, "Isn't this just for accountants or adults?"

But the truth is, the earlier you learn to measure your money, the more confident and in control you'll feel.

A balance sheet helps you:

- Understand the real value of your money and belongings
- Stay organized with both savings and debts
- Make clear, informed financial choices instead of random ones
- Avoid the trap of spending more than you actually have
- Start building wealth step by step, even at a young age

Most adults never practice this. They spend, borrow, and hope for the best. But you? You're learning to measure your money like a builder measures bricks—piece by piece, until it forms something solid.

Keeping Your Own Balance Sheet

You don't need fancy software to start.

Just use a notebook or a simple spreadsheet. Create three sections:

1. Assets: List everything you own that has value.
2. Liabilities: List what you owe to others.
3. Net Worth: Subtract liabilities from assets.

Update it once a month. Track your changes. Watch how your net worth moves over time.

Seeing your money story written out gives you clarity and power—because you know exactly where you stand.

Recap

In this chapter, you learned:

- A balance sheet is your personal money scoreboard.
- Assets are the things you own that carry value.
- Liabilities are debts or amounts you owe to others.
- Net worth = assets minus liabilities.
- Tracking your balance sheet helps you stay organized and grow stronger financially.

In the next chapter, we'll explore something even more dynamic: cash flow—how money moves in and out of your hands. Understanding that is like learning the rhythm of your financial life.

Key Points:

- Your personal financial scoreboard.
- Assets are things you own.
- Liabilities are things you owe.
- Net worth equals assets minus liabilities.
- Example: Fifty dollars savings + ten-dollar IOU – five dollars owed = fifty-five net worth.
- Visuals: A simple balance sheet table and two jars labeled "Assets" and "Liabilities."

Chapter 5:
The Income and Expense Statement

Okay, imagine this.

You just earned twenty bucks for helping your neighbor clean out their garage. Instantly, you feel rich. In your head, you're already building a shopping list: a bag full of snacks, maybe that new Roblox skin, and of course the five-dollar boba drink everyone's been raving about. Fast-forward just two days later—you check your pockets, and you're broke. Again. The worst part? You can't even explain where it all went.

That's what happens when money isn't tracked. It slips away quietly, like a magician's rabbit vanishing into thin air. Poof.

So how do we stop that from happening?

By learning about something that sounds complicated but is actually a game-changer: the Income and Expense Statement.

What Is It, Really?

Don't let the name intimidate you. At its core, it's just a structured way of saying:

"Write down how much money you made, how much you spent, and what's left over."

That's it. But here's why it matters: this simple process transforms money from being a mystery into something you can control. Without a record, you're guessing. With a record, you're managing.

Think of it like keeping score in a game. You wouldn't play basketball without tracking the points, right? The income and expense statement is your financial scoreboard.

Why Should You Care?

Because money behaves like water. If you don't have a container, it leaks everywhere. You could earn a million dollars, but if you spend a million and one, you're not rich—you're in debt.

And here's the key: the income and expense statement *is your container*. It gives your money boundaries and helps you see clearly whether it's building up or draining out.

Robert Kiyosaki, author of *Rich Dad Poor Dad*, puts it perfectly:

"It's not how much money you make. It's how much money you keep."

That's the difference between financial growth and financial frustration. Some people make a lot and still end up with nothing. Others earn modestly but track, manage, and grow their money.

Which side do you want to be on?

Breaking Down the Statement

At its simplest, the income and expense statement has three key parts:

1. Income → Money coming in. This could be allowance, birthday cash, lemonade stand profits, babysitting money, tutoring pay, or payments for mowing lawns.
2. Expenses → Money going out. Think snacks, online games, subscriptions, clothes, toys, or random Amazon buys.
3. Profit (or Loss) → What's left after subtracting expenses from income.

Here's the formula:

Profit = Income – Expenses

Examples:

- If you earn $30 and spend $25, you've got $5 left. That's a profit.
- If you earn $20 but spend $22, you're at –$2. That's a loss.

The goal? Stay positive. It's not just about making money—it's about *keeping it.*

Story Time: Meet Jayden, the Snack King

Jayden was 13. Every week, he received a $15 allowance and earned another $10 selling gum at school. That gave him $25 per week—around $100 a month.

But Jayden never tracked his money. Every Friday, he'd drop $6 on pizza, $5 on a new skin, and a few bucks here and there on candy, sodas, or gadgets.

He thought he was doing fine.

Then his cousin—an older teen who had read *Rich Dad Poor Dad*—asked him, "Bro, you've been making a hundred dollars a month. Where is it?"

Jayden shrugged. "I guess I spent it."

His cousin pulled out a notebook and introduced him to the income and expense sheet.

Jayden's weekly breakdown looked like this:

Income:

- $15 allowance
- $10 gum sales
  Total: $25

Expenses:

- $6 pizza
- $5 app skin
- $7 snacks
- $8 random gadget
  Total: $26

Net Profit: $25 − $26 = −$1

Jayden wasn't just spending all his money—he was overspending. And until he saw the numbers written down, he had no idea.

His cousin explained:

"The danger of not tracking your money is that it's easy to lie to yourself. You think you're doing fine, but you're not."

That moment flipped a switch for Jayden.

A Rich Dad vs. Poor Dad Lesson

Robert Kiyosaki often contrasts two mindsets:

- His "Poor Dad" believed that simply earning more money solved everything.
- His "Rich Dad" knew that managing money was more important than just making it.

The income and expense statement is step one in building that "Rich Dad" mindset. It forces you to see the truth of your habits, good or bad, so you can adjust.

Another Story: Sarah's Pet Sitting Side Hustle

Sarah was 12 and loved animals. She offered pet sitting in her neighborhood—$10 for a walk, $15 for overnight care. In just two months, she made $120.

But she also loved bubble tea, online games, and plushies. At the end of two months, she had only $5 left.

When she finally tracked her numbers, here's what she discovered:

- $45 spent on drinks
- $30 on games
- $40 on toys

Her parents helped her color-code her expenses: green for useful spending, red for "wants." Seeing her statement filled with red was a shock.

That's when she made a decision: instead of draining her earnings, she'd save for a bike trailer so she could walk *two dogs at once*. More income, less waste.

For Sarah, tracking revealed the link between habits and goals. That's the power of this tool.

What Happens When You Start Tracking?

1. You find money leaks. You might be shocked at how much disappears into "little things."
2. You build habits with evidence. Tracking removes guesswork, like counting calories helps with health.
3. You feel empowered. Seeing every dollar gives you control. You become the boss.
4. You move closer to your goals. Whether it's a phone, a bike, or your first investment—tracking makes progress visible.

Real Talk: Most Adults Don't Even Do This

Here's the secret: most adults skip this step. They just hope the money lasts until the end of the month.

But not you. By learning this now, you're ahead.

Robert Kiyosaki once said:

"The single most powerful asset we all have is our mind. If it is trained well, it can create enormous wealth."

Tracking your money is part of that training.

Simple Ways to Start Tracking (Without Falling Asleep)

1. Notebook + Ruler → Draw a line: income on one side, expenses on the other.
2. Index Cards → Make a fresh one each week and carry it with you.
3. Phone Notes or Apps → Use your Notes app or a simple budgeting app.
4. Gamify It → Compete with a sibling or friend. Who saved more?

Mistakes to Avoid

- Forgetting the "little stuff." Even $1–$2 expenses add up.
- Waiting too long to log it. "I'll remember later" = forgotten.
- Rounding numbers. Don't fudge the math. Be honest.

Your future self will thank you.

Recap

- Income = money in
- Expenses = money out
- Profit = what's left
- Track it weekly
- No guessing. No lying. Just the truth.
- Tracking turns money into a tool, not a stress.

You're the CFO of You

Big companies hire CFOs—Chief Financial Officers—to manage money, keep the company alive, and make it grow.

Well, guess what? You're the CFO of your life.

That notebook, spreadsheet, or app? That's not just paper or pixels. That's your blueprint for financial freedom.

Key Points

- Track your money flow
- Income = money in
- Expenses = money out
- Profit = Income – Expenses
- Example: Earn $30, spend $25 → $5 profit
- Visuals: Bar graph showing income vs. expenses + sample income/expense table.

Chapter 6:
Cash Flow Statement

Imagine you're playing Monopoly, rolling dice, buying properties, collecting rent — but you never keep track of your money. You don't know if you're winning, losing, or flat-out broke. You're just guessing.

That's exactly what life feels like if you don't track *cash flow*.

Most kids (and honestly, most adults) know about a *balance sheet* — the list of what you own (assets) and what you owe (liabilities). That's like taking a snapshot of your money at one exact moment.

But money doesn't just sit still like a photo. It moves. It flows. And that's where the *cash flow statement* comes in.

What Even *Is* Cash Flow?

Cash flow is just a fancy way of saying:

- Money flowing in when you earn.
- Money flowing out when you spend.

Think of it like breathing. Inhaling is money coming in. Exhaling is money going out. If you only exhale and never inhale, well… you run out of breath. Same with money — if you spend without earning, you're in trouble.

A balance sheet = still photo. A cash flow statement = video in motion.

Breaking It Down: Cash In vs. Cash Out

Two main parts keep this simple:

1. Cash Inflows: All the ways money enters your life — allowance, side hustles, birthday money, selling stuff you don't use, or even interest from savings.
2. Cash Outflows: All the ways money leaves — snacks, video games, subscriptions, rides with friends, or paying someone back.

Now, put them together:

Cash Flow = Cash In − Cash Out

- If the number is positive, awesome. Your money is stacking up.
- If the number is negative, uh-oh. You're spending more than you're earning.

Rich Dad vs. Poor Dad: A Tale of Two Mindsets

Robert Kiyosaki grew up with two father figures:

- Poor Dad: His real father. Smart, well-educated, always said, "Go to school, get good grades, and find a safe job." But here's the problem: he spent everything he earned. His cash flow leaked like a broken pipe.
- Rich Dad: His best friend's father. Not as educated on paper, but wise with money. He believed, *"The rich don't work for money. They make money work for them."*

How? By focusing on assets that generate positive cash flow.

The Classic Lesson: The House That Eats vs. The House That Feeds

When Robert asked if a big house was an investment, here's how the dads answered:

- Poor Dad: Bought a large home. Every month it sucked money away in mortgage, taxes, and repairs. It looked fancy, but it drained cash. That's a liability.
- Rich Dad: Bought a modest home. With his extra money, he bought rental properties. Every month, those tenants paid him. That's an asset. His house fed him instead of eating away his money.

Robert's takeaway: *"An asset is something that puts money in your pocket. A liability takes money out."*

A Kid-Friendly Example: The Bike vs. the Hoverboard

Let's compare two kids:

- Leo's Delivery Bike: Leo saves up and buys a sturdy bike. He uses it to deliver groceries for neighbors, making $10–15 a week. The bike cost money at first, but now it *brings* money in. That's positive cash flow.
- Sam's Hoverboard: Sam buys a flashy hoverboard. It's fun, sure — until it breaks and needs new parts. It never earns him a cent, only drains his wallet. That's negative cash flow.

Same starting point (money to spend), but two very different outcomes.

Why Cash Flow Is the Real Superpower

A lot of people think being rich means just having money in the bank. But here's the secret:

Rich people don't just save. They set up systems where money keeps flowing in, even when they're not working.

Examples of cash inflows that never stop:

- Rent from a house
- Dividends from stocks
- Royalties from a book, song, or game design
- Profits from a business

Meanwhile, someone with a good job but equally high expenses? Their cash flow is zero — or worse, negative.

Your Personal Cash Flow Tracker

Ready to start? Keep it simple with three sections:

1. Cash In – Every dollar you earn or receive
2. Cash Out – Every dollar you spend
3. Net Cash Flow – Subtract #2 from #1

Do this for a week or a month and watch patterns appear:

- That $5 snack every other day? Adds up fast.
- That old toy you sold for $20? Extra inflow you can use.

Tracking = awareness. Awareness = control.

Your Money Moves — Make It Dance

Cash flow is motion. It's not about how much you have sitting in a jar — it's about how your money travels.

You can either let it wander off without you noticing, or you can become the choreographer. Make it move where you want.

The key question isn't: *"How much money do I have?"*

It's: *"How well is my money working for me?"*

Key Points Recap

- Balance sheet = snapshot.
- Cash flow = money in motion.
- Rich Dad mindset: buy assets that generate income.
- Poor Dad mindset: buy liabilities that drain money.
- Example: A delivery bike earns (asset). A hoverboard costs (liability).
- Tools: Use a simple tracker to monitor inflows vs. outflows.
- Visuals: Cash flow diagram + sample cash flow sheet.

Chapter 7:
Assets Make You Rich

What if I told you that money doesn't make you rich?

Sounds strange, right? But it's true. Just having money doesn't mean you'll stay wealthy. What really makes people rich is owning things that keep earning more money — even while you sleep, eat, or play video games.

Those money-makers have a name: assets.

Let's dig into how the rich build wealth — not just by working hard, but by making their money work hard for them.

Working for Money vs. Making Money Work

Meet Jake and Maya.

- Jake mows lawns on weekends. Every lawn gets him twenty bucks. After five lawns, he's made a hundred dollars. Awesome — but the second Jake stops mowing, the cash stops flowing.
- **Maya** used her birthday money to buy a vending machine with her dad's help. They placed it in her uncle's garage shop. Every week she refills it with snacks, and every week it spits out about fifteen dollars — whether Maya's at school, asleep, or watching movies.

Jake works for money.

Maya owns an asset that works for her.

That's the key lesson: *Assets = money that works for you.*

What Are Assets?

Assets are things that put money into your pocket. They don't just sit there; they grow, pay, or create value.

Examples of assets include:

- A rental property that gives monthly rent
- A vending machine that earns snack money
- A stock that pays dividends
- A small business that turns profit
- Even a rare comic book that increases in value over time

In *Rich Dad Poor Dad,* Robert Kiyosaki explains: the rich focus on building assets first. They don't race to buy the flashiest stuff. Instead, they grow their "asset machine" — a collection of things that quietly make them richer every day.

What Are Liabilities?

Liabilities are the opposite of assets. Instead of putting money in your pocket, they take money out.

Think about:

- A fancy phone with an expensive monthly plan
- A car that eats money for gas and repairs
- Designer shoes that look great but drain your savings
- A video game console that collects dust after a few weeks

Fun? Sure. But the more you pile them up, the further they pull you away from wealth.

The real trap? Many people think they're buying assets when they're actually buying liabilities.

Example: A huge house might *look* like an asset. But if the mortgage, taxes, and repairs cost more than it earns, it's a liability in disguise.

Kiyosaki sums it up perfectly: *"The rich buy assets. The poor only have expenses. The middle class buys liabilities they think are assets."*

Read that again. That's the wake-up call.

Your Brain: The Ultimate Asset

Here's something most people overlook — you are your biggest asset.

Every time you read a book like this, ask money questions, or practice financial thinking, you're upgrading your brain. And unlike sneakers or phones, knowledge never wears out.

That's why the wealthy invest in education, mentors, and training. They know building brainpower pays dividends for life.

Building Your Asset Machine

Think of each asset as a little worker you hire. The more workers you have, the more they bring in — even when you're not around.

Here's how to start building:

1. You earn money.
2. You save a chunk of it.
3. You buy or build an asset.
4. That asset makes more money.
5. You use that money to buy *more* assets.

Soon, your money army is working harder than you are.

Some starter ideas:

- Buy a used gumball machine for a family friend's shop.
- Create a digital comic series and sell each issue for $1.
- Use allowance to launch a lemonade stand with your sibling.
- Save up for a dividend-paying stock.

Start small. Grow steady. Watch the machine get stronger.

Rich Dad vs. Poor Dad: The Real Lesson

Robert had two dads.

- Poor Dad: Brilliant teacher. Worked hard for a salary. Believed in promotions, paychecks, and stability. But he stayed stuck trading time for money.
- Rich Dad: Not as formally educated. But he focused on assets — businesses, rentals, investments. Money worked *for him.*

The turning point for Robert wasn't a new job. It was understanding that wealth is built on assets, not paychecks.

A Story: The Toy That Paid Me Back

When I was eight, I wanted a remote-control car more than anything. My cousin had one, and I felt left out.

Instead of spending my savings, I used them to start selling handmade keychains at school events. Two dollars each, all shapes and colors. Pretty soon, kids were requesting custom ones. In three months, I'd made more than enough for the car.

But here's the twist: I didn't buy it.

I reinvested the money into more supplies. Then I teamed up with a friend who had a label printer, and we launched a mini sticker business. Together, we sold hundreds.

That car? I never got it. But I built my first asset. And it's still one of the most valuable lessons I've ever learned.

What Will Your First Asset Be?

Your first asset doesn't need to be huge. It just needs to *work.*

Maybe it's:

- A digital product
- A vending machine
- A small investment account
- A side hustle that grows over time

The point is this: assets build wealth, liabilities drain it.

So the next time you spend, save, or invest, pause and ask:

Does this make me richer, or just look cool for a minute?

Choose the long game. Choose assets.

Key Points Recap

- Assets put money in your pocket.
- Liabilities take money out.
- Build your "asset machine" one step at a time.
- Example: A gumball machine earns money; designer shoes don't.
- Visual: Side-by-side chart of assets vs. liabilities.

Chapter 8:
Your First Financial Goal

Let's get real for a second.

You've learned a lot about money by now. You've seen how earning, spending, saving, and investing all fit together. You know the difference between assets and liabilities. But here's the catch: knowledge without action doesn't change much. It's like knowing how to ride a bike but never pedaling forward.

This chapter is about the next big step: setting your first real financial goal.

A goal gives direction. Without one, money just comes and goes. With one, you start building something solid.

So let's break down what a financial goal is, how to choose a smart one, and how to reach it—step by step.

What Is a Financial Goal?

A financial goal is something you want to achieve that involves money. Simple enough.

It can be big or small. Short-term or long-term. Something for fun or something for your future.

The difference is this: it's not just a wish. It's a plan.

Wishing sits still. Goal-setting moves forward.

Examples of financial goals:

- Save fifty dollars to buy a skateboard
- Earn one hundred dollars to start a sticker business
- Buy your first dividend-paying stock
- Raise two hundred dollars to donate to a cause
- Set aside money for a summer coding camp

Different as they are, they all do the same thing: they give your money a mission.

And money with a mission becomes powerful.

Why Most People Don't Set Goals

Surprisingly, a lot of adults don't set financial goals. Some are nervous. Some don't know how. Others avoid thinking about money altogether.

Here's what usually gets in the way:

- They think it's too complicated
- They're afraid of failing
- They believe they don't have "enough" to start
- They were never taught how

But you're different. You're learning early. And the best way to use that knowledge is to put it into practice.

The Power of a Specific Goal

Vague goals don't work.

Saying "I want to be rich" is like saying "I want to go somewhere cool." Where? When? How?

Now compare that to: "I want to earn seventy-five dollars in two months by selling custom digital art prints online so I can buy a new drawing tablet."

That's specific. That's a map.

The clearer your goal, the easier it is to see the next step.

Step 1: Pick Something That Excites You

Your first financial goal shouldn't feel like homework. It should spark excitement. Maybe it's fun, maybe it's generous, maybe it moves you forward.

The best goals are ones you actually care about.

Want a new mountain bike? That counts. Want to buy your first share of stock? Perfect. Want to save for a trip to see your grandparents? Great.

Don't choose what "sounds responsible." Choose what feels real.

Step 2: Decide on a Target Number

Every goal needs a number.

If the keyboard costs eighty dollars, that's your target. If you want to raise one hundred for charity, that's the mark. Even with investing, start with a clear figure—maybe twenty-five or fifty dollars.

Your brain likes clear.

Step 3: Set a Deadline

Goals without deadlines drift into "someday." And someday often becomes never.

So set a time frame. Three weeks? A month? Three months?

Make it realistic—but not so far away that you lose momentum.

Step 4: Break It Down

Big numbers can feel heavy. Breaking them down makes them manageable.

If you want seventy dollars in seven weeks, that's ten dollars a week.

Can you mow a lawn, sell lemonade, make bracelets, or do a chore for ten bucks? Probably. Suddenly, the big goal shrinks into something doable.

Step 5: Track It

Grab a notebook, chart, or whiteboard. Write your goal at the top and track your progress underneath.

Every time you earn or save, mark it down.

Now your goal becomes a game—and who doesn't like leveling up?

A Story: My First Financial Goal Wasn't About Money

When I was ten, I wanted to go to a science camp out of town. A week with robots, rockets, and everything I loved. But it cost one hundred and fifty dollars.

My parents said, "We'll pay half. You raise the other half."

At first, I thought that was unfair. But then I saw the opportunity.

I made a flyer offering "backyard cleanup" for five bucks—raking leaves, sweeping patios, picking up sticks. Boring? Sure. But I teamed up with my cousin, played music while we worked, and even added a tip jar.

In five weeks, I had my seventy-five dollars.

At camp, while launching a rocket I helped build, it hit me: I didn't just buy a ticket. I built it.

That stuck. Because money isn't just about stuff. It's about ownership. It's about freedom.

That goal was my first taste of both.

Different Kinds of Goals

Financial goals don't all have to be about buying things. Some of the best goals are about habits or skills.

Examples:

- Save a set amount every week for a year
- Create a spreadsheet to track expenses
- Earn your first ten dollars without asking parents
- Start a tiny business and make your first sale
- Learn how to use a budgeting app
- Save enough to buy your first asset

They may not look flashy, but they build financial muscle.

A Quick Note on Failing

Sometimes you'll miss a goal. Life happens.

Here's the key: don't stop.

Missing a goal doesn't mean failure. It means feedback.

Reset. Adjust the deadline. Change the method. But keep going.

Every retry builds confidence.

Make It Visible

Put your goal where you can see it.

On a poster. A sticky note on your mirror. Your phone wallpaper.

Each glance is a reminder: this is where you're headed.

Your First Goal Can Be Small, But It Won't Stay Small

Say your first goal is saving twenty dollars for craft supplies.

Seems tiny.

But what happens when that craft business makes you forty?

Now you've got a new goal: expand it. Use the money to create more. Save some. Maybe invest.

You're not just reaching goals—you're stacking them.

Like climbing stairs: one step at a time, higher and higher.

The Real Win: Ownership and Confidence

Even more important than the money is the feeling of hitting a goal.

You start believing you can do hard things. You stop waiting for permission. You think like the CEO of your own life.

You're not just saving. You're building.

So... What's Your First Goal?

Grab a piece of paper and write it down right now:

- What do you want?

- How much does it cost?
- By when do you want it?
- How will you get there?

Start there.

Because once you take that first step, you're not just learning about money—you're using it.

Key Points:

- Money without a purpose disappears
- Set short-term and long-term goals
- Saving plans help you say yes later
- Mini-story: Saving for a camera to launch a YouTube channel
- Visuals: Goal tracker and weekly savings plan with a progress bar

Chapter 9:
Be the CEO of You Inc

Have you ever heard someone say, "You're just a kid"? Like being young somehow means you're not important or in charge of anything? Let's flip that idea. You're already in charge of something huge—yourself.

Think of your life as a business. You have time, energy, ideas, and money. And just like a business must manage its resources, make smart choices, and grow, so must you.

Let's call this business *You Inc.* And guess what? You're the CEO.

What Does a CEO Do?

A CEO (Chief Executive Officer) leads a company. They don't handle every single task, but they make the key decisions. They set goals, design strategies, and guide their team toward success.

As the CEO of *You Inc.*, you're doing the same thing—but with your own life.

Instead of managing a company that sells sneakers or apps, you're managing your time, your money, your knowledge, and your future.

Every time you choose to save instead of spend, you're acting like a CEO. Every time you learn a new skill, you're investing in your company—yourself.

Money Decisions Are Business Decisions

In business, you can't blow all your cash on fun and hope things turn out fine. You plan. You know what's coming in and what's going out.

Say you get ten dollars a week for allowance. A typical kid might spend it all right away. But the CEO of *You Inc.* stops and asks:

- Do I want to spend all of this now?
- Can I set some aside to invest in myself?
- What could I build with this money instead of just buying something?

Maybe you spend two dollars on a treat and save the other eight. Over time, those savings grow into power. Money saved becomes money that can multiply. That's CEO thinking.

You Inc Has a Budget

Businesses run on budgets. You should too. A personal budget doesn't need to be complicated. It just needs to show three things:

1. Income – What's coming in
2. Expenses – What's going out
3. Savings & Investing – What's left and how you'll use it

Example:

Weekly Income:

- Allowance: $10

- Dog walking: $5
- Total: $15

Weekly Expenses:

- Snack from store: $3
- Arcade games: $2
- Total: $5

Leftover for savings and investing: $10

That leftover is where growth happens. You can put it toward books, tools, a side hustle, or even an asset—something that earns money later.

Use Your Time Like a Boss

Good CEOs don't just manage money. They manage time. You get the same 24 hours as everyone else, but how you spend them changes your future.

Ask yourself:

- How much time am I watching videos versus learning?
- Could I trade one hour of screen time for one hour on a business idea?
- What skill could I practice today that my future self will thank me for?

Time is one of your most valuable assets. Waste it, and it's gone. Use it wisely, and it multiplies your opportunities.

Invest in Yourself

The smartest CEOs invest in their people. And *You Inc.* has one person—you.

That might look like:

1. Reading books on business, money, or creativity
2. Watching videos that teach real skills
3. Taking on challenges that stretch you
4. Starting a side hustle, even if tiny

Robert Kiyosaki said, "The most important investment you can make is in yourself." Every skill learned, every bit of confidence gained, is an upgrade for your business.

Track Your Progress

Companies track growth with reports—sales, profits, goals. You should do the same.

Ways to track *You Inc.*:

- Keep a journal of earnings and expenses
- Write down monthly goals and check them off
- Create a "learning log" to record skills you're building

Tracking reveals patterns. Maybe you save more when you make a plan. Maybe you're spending on things that don't really make you happy. Knowledge is power—if you use it.

Build Your Personal Brand

Every successful business has a brand. It's what people think of first. *You Inc.* has one too.

What are you known for? Being dependable, creative, hardworking, curious? Do you finish what you start? Do you ask sharp questions?

That's your personal brand—your silent message to the world. It shapes the opportunities you get, the way people treat you, and how much you believe in yourself.

You don't need to be perfect. You just need to keep growing.

Real CEOs Make Mistakes

Here's the truth: CEOs mess up all the time. But they don't quit. They learn, adjust, and keep moving.

If you overspend one week, don't panic. Review it, figure out why, and try again.

Say you start a lemonade stand and lose money because you bought too many lemons. That's not failure—it's feedback. Next time, you'll buy less, or add new products to boost sales.

You Inc. is always learning.

Think Bigger Than Today

Good CEOs plan beyond the moment. You should too.

Ask yourself:

- Where do I want to be in a year? Five years?
- What will I wish I had started today?
- How can I create more opportunities?

Dream of being a game designer? Start small. Learn how games are made, sketch your own ideas, save for development tools. Every small step compounds.

One day, you'll see your progress came from the choices you made as CEO of *You Inc.*

Your Board of Advisors

Even top CEOs don't do it alone. They lean on advisors. You can too.

Your "board" might be:

- A parent or grandparent who gives money advice
- A teacher who develops your talents
- A hardworking friend who inspires you
- A YouTuber or author who teaches great lessons

Surround yourself with people who make you stronger, and your decisions improve.

So… Are You Ready to Lead?

You don't need to wait until adulthood to run your life like a business. The earlier you start, the stronger you'll be.

Be smart with money.

Use time like it matters—because it does.

Make mistakes, learn, and move forward.

Act like a CEO, even when no one's watching.

You Inc. is open for business. And the future? It's all yours.

Key Points:

- You're not just a kid—you're a business of your own
- Track income and treat savings like capital
- Invest your time like a boss
- Example: Managing allowance like a CEO
- Visual: A kid at a desk with a budget, calculator, and lightbulb labeled "CEO of M"

Chapter 10:
What Are Stocks

Imagine if you could own a tiny slice of your favorite companies — a bit of Nike, Roblox, or Apple? And what if those companies paid you money just for owning that slice? That's what stocks are. They're like little tickets proving you own part of a company. And the right ones can help you build real wealth over time.

Stocks might sound complicated, but once you get the basics (and a little advanced stuff), they're one of the most exciting tools in your money journey. This chapter will show you how stocks work, why they rise or fall, how to read them, and how they can make you money even while you sleep.

Rich Dad said: *"The rich focus on buying assets. The poor and middle class acquire liabilities they think are assets."*

Stocks can be one of the strongest assets you own — but only if you understand them.

What Exactly Is a Stock?

When a company wants to grow — open stores, launch a new game, invent a product — it needs cash. One way is by selling shares of the company to the public. Buy a share, and you own a small piece of that company. That piece is called a stock.

Example: Imagine a lemonade brand called *Sunny Sips*. It's worth $1 million and splits itself into one million shares. Each share is worth $1. If you buy 10 shares, you own 10 out of one million parts of Sunny Sips. That makes you a shareholder.

Why Own a Stock?

Because when the company grows, so does your piece of it.

If *Sunny Sips* doubles in value to $2 million, each share jumps from $1 to $2. Your $10 investment is now worth $20.

And sometimes, companies even share profits with investors through dividends — a small payout just for being a shareholder.

Two Ways to Make Money with Stocks

1. Capital appreciation — the stock price climbs, and you sell for more than you paid.
2. Dividends — steady payments from the company, often every three months.

Not all companies pay dividends. Startups usually reinvest earnings to grow bigger, while established firms like banks or utilities often pay steady dividends.

But remember: just as stocks can go up, they can also fall.

Why Do Prices Change?

Stock prices rise and drop because of supply and demand. More buyers push prices up; more sellers push prices down.

What drives those choices?

- Company performance — earnings, products, or mistakes.
- News — launches, scandals, leadership changes.
- Economy — inflation, interest rates, government policy.
- Emotions — fear and greed drive a lot of buying and selling.

Rich Dad said: *"The market is driven by fear and greed."*

Smart investors don't just follow hype — they study the numbers.

Key Numbers to Know

P/E Ratio (Price-to-Earnings)

- A stock at $100 making $10 per share = P/E of 10.
- Higher P/E = more expensive (or high growth expected).
- Lower P/E = possibly undervalued (or risky).

Think of it like buying a vending machine:

- If it earns $10 a year and costs $100, that's a P/E of 10 — it takes 10 years to earn back.
- If it earns only $5, the P/E is 20 — it takes longer.

Market Cap (Company Size) = Stock price × number of shares.

- Small-cap: $300M–$2B (fast growth, riskier).
- Mid-cap: $2B–$10B (steady balance).

- Large-cap: $10B+ (big and stable).

Beta (Bounciness)

Measures how much a stock moves compared to the market.

- Beta 1.0 = same as market.
- Beta 1.5 = more volatile.
- Beta 0.5 = calmer, less risky.

High beta = big swings (risk/reward). Low beta = steady but slower.

Types of Stocks

- Growth stocks — reinvest profits to grow fast (usually no dividends).
- Value stocks — strong but underpriced companies.
- Dividend stocks — reliable payouts, like rental income.
- Blue chips — big, trusted companies like Apple or Coca-Cola.
- Penny stocks — super cheap, very risky, often avoided.

Stock Indexes

Instead of tracking one company, indexes measure groups:

- S&P 500 — 500 of the biggest U.S. companies.
- Dow Jones — 30 large, mixed companies.
- Nasdaq — mostly tech.

If the S&P 500 is up, it usually means the market overall is strong.

How Can Kids Start Learning?

Even if you can't invest real money yet, you can practice:

- Track companies you like.
- Pretend-buy a few shares and watch them.
- Keep a stock journal of "fake" trades and lessons.
- Use simulators or apps to practice.

By the time you can invest real money, you'll already have skills most adults don't.

Real-Life Story: Rich Dad's Lesson

In *Rich Dad Poor Dad,* Robert Kiyosaki shared how his rich dad taught him to study companies. He read reports, learned about earnings and debt, and figured out which firms had strong cash flow.

Instead of guessing, he built knowledge — and it paid off. One of his early stock picks doubled, not by luck, but by research.

Most people buy iPhones. Investors buy Apple stock.

Final Thoughts

Stocks aren't magic or gambling. They're tools for building wealth if you're patient and informed. They let you own a piece of companies shaping the world.

The secret isn't luck — it's learning, practicing, and thinking like an investor.

And the best time to start? Right now.

Key Points:

- Stocks = tiny ownership slices of companies.
- Prices change with performance, news, and emotions.
- Two money paths: capital appreciation + dividends.
- Tools: P/E, market cap, beta.
- Types: growth, value, dividend, blue chip, penny.
- Kids can practice with "pretend portfolios" before investing for real.
- Visual: A pie chart showing company ownership slices.

Chapter 11:
What Is Real Estate

Imagine this: You're walking down a street and see a giant red-brick building with a "For Sale" sign out front. Across the street sits a small park, surrounded by houses, a grocery store, and a coffee shop. All of this — the land, the structures, the homes, and even the commercial spaces — falls under the umbrella of real estate.

Real estate isn't just about buying a home or becoming a landlord. It's about understanding how land and property can function as wealth-building instruments. For centuries, people have used property as one of the most reliable vehicles for financial growth.

Robert Kiyosaki, in *Rich Dad Poor Dad*, highlights a key distinction: wealthy people purchase assets that generate income, while the poor often purchase liabilities that drain it. Real estate, when approached correctly, is one of those income-producing assets. That simple difference in mindset changes everything.

So, let's take a closer look at how real estate works — not just as a place to live, but as a system where money flows through property and grows over time.

What Counts As Real Estate?

Real estate isn't a single category. It comes in many forms, each with its own opportunities and challenges:

- Residential real estate: Houses, apartments, condos, and any property where people live.

- Commercial real estate: Office buildings, retail stores, restaurants, and malls where businesses operate.
- Industrial real estate: Factories, warehouses, and production facilities used for manufacturing and storage.
- Raw land: Undeveloped property that may serve agricultural purposes now or later be developed into homes, businesses, or industrial sites.

At its core, real estate is simply land and anything permanently attached to it. But each category functions differently, generates money differently, and carries different risks. That's where the strategy comes in.

How does real estate make money?

There are two primary wealth-building mechanisms in real estate:

1. Rental income – Payments made by tenants who occupy your property. For example, if you own a duplex and each unit rents for $1,000 per month, that's $2,000 in gross rental income. It's almost like the building itself is your employee, earning while you sleep.
2. Appreciation – The increase in property value over time. Buy a plot of land for $10,000, and if five years later someone offers $20,000, you've doubled your money without lifting a finger.

When combined, these two streams — steady rental income plus long-term appreciation — can create a powerful wealth engine.

Don't Forget Expenses

Of course, property ownership comes with costs: maintenance, property taxes, insurance, and often a mortgage. That's why investors track cash flow, which is income minus expenses.

If your property earns $1,200 in rent but costs you $800 to maintain, your net cash flow is $400. That positive cash flow is the lifeblood of sustainable investing. Negative cash flow, on the other hand, means your property is costing you money to keep — making it more of a liability than an asset.

A tale of two brothers

Consider two fictional brothers, Leo and Max. Both inherit $20,000.

- Leo spends his inheritance on a new car, a vacation, and designer clothes. Within six months, the money is gone, and all he has left are depreciating possessions.
- Max uses his $20,000 as a down payment on a small duplex in a town that's slowly expanding. After renovating it, he rents both units, bringing in $700 per month per unit. After subtracting expenses, he nets $400 per month in positive cash flow.

In just one year, Max has nearly $5,000 in profit and still owns an appreciating property. Over time, he can use that equity to purchase more real estate, creating a chain of growth.

The contrast is simple: Leo consumed wealth; Max created wealth.

The Concept Of Leverage

One of the most powerful tools in real estate is leverage — using borrowed money to control a valuable asset.

Suppose you want to buy a $100,000 property. Instead of paying the full amount in cash, you put down $20,000 and finance the rest through a bank loan. You now own the entire property but only committed a fraction of your own money.

If the property's value rises to $150,000, your return on the original $20,000 investment is not 50 percent but 150 percent. That's the multiplying effect of leverage.

But leverage is double-edged: if property values drop or rental income falters, debt can magnify losses just as easily as gains. Smart investors balance opportunity with risk.

Why Location Matters

There's an old saying in real estate: *location, location, location.* It means geography often outweighs the property itself.

- A small home in a growing city can be worth more than a mansion in a declining town.
- A shop on a bustling main street can outperform a beautiful storefront tucked away in a quiet neighborhood.

Investors study trends like migration, job creation, schools, infrastructure, and even zoning changes to predict where values will rise. Good location decisions often separate winning investments from losing ones.

Real Estate vs. Stocks

Why invest in property when you could buy stocks? Both are valid paths, but they differ in structure:

- Stocks: Highly liquid, easy to buy or sell, and simple to diversify with small amounts of money.
- Real estate: Requires more upfront capital and active management but offers steady income, potential tax advantages, and more control over outcomes.

Many successful investors combine both, using stocks for rapid liquidity and growth while relying on real estate for stability and cash flow.

Escaping the Rat Race

In *Rich Dad Poor Dad*, Kiyosaki describes the "Rat Race": working paycheck to paycheck, always chasing bills. Real estate provides a potential exit.

If you own enough rental properties producing positive cash flow, you don't have to trade time for money anymore. The properties generate income whether you work or not — shifting you from financial survival to financial freedom.

The math behind real estate

Investors don't rely only on instinct. They use key financial metrics:

- Cap Rate (Capitalization Rate): Annual income ÷ property price. A $100,000 property generating $10,000 per year has a 10% cap rate.

- Cash-on-Cash Return: Annual cash flow ÷ initial investment. If you invest $20,000 and earn $2,000 annually, that's a 10% return.
- Vacancy Rate: The percentage of time a property is unoccupied. High vacancies cut into profits, so location and demand matter.

These formulas bring discipline to decisions, ensuring choices are based on numbers, not emotions.

The reality of real estate

Property ownership isn't effortless. Investors face maintenance headaches, tenant disputes, unexpected repairs, and shifting markets. There will be setbacks.

But unlike speculative ventures, real estate has staying power. With patience and knowledge, properties can steadily generate income and accumulate value, rewarding those who play the long game.

Key Points Recap

- Real estate includes land, homes, apartments, and buildings of all kinds.
- Money is earned through rental income and appreciation.
- Real estate can be an asset when it generates positive cash flow.
- Example: A lemonade stand buys a corner lot, rents space to other vendors, and collects rent.
- Visual: Diagram showing property → tenants → rent → cash flow.

Chapter 12:
Risk and Reward

Imagine you're standing on the edge of a diving board. Beneath you is a pool. It's deep enough to jump into, but your stomach still twists. You don't know exactly what will happen. Will it be exhilarating? Will the height overwhelm you? Will you land smoothly or belly flop? That feeling—that cocktail of excitement and unease—is what people call risk. Yet if you leap and land well, the splash and thrill become the reward.

This balance between risk and reward is one of the most important lessons in money. Nearly every financial decision—whether investing, starting a business, or even choosing where to place your savings—revolves around it.

Most people want big rewards. But far fewer are willing to accept big risks. That's why learning how to manage risk wisely—rather than avoiding it entirely—is one of the most powerful money skills you can develop.

What Is Risk?

Risk is the chance that things won't go the way you expect.

In financial terms, risk means the possibility of losing money or falling short of the return you anticipated. Higher risk raises the chance of failure, but also raises the possibility of exceptional gain.

Think of it as a spectrum, a sliding scale. On one end sits low-risk behavior, like keeping money in a piggy bank.

On the other end lies high-risk behavior, like investing in an untested app nobody's heard of.

The key insight: avoiding risk entirely may protect you in the short term, but it also caps your potential. Smart investors learn to manage risk—not hide from it.

What Is Reward?

Reward is what you gain when things go right. In finance, it usually translates into profit, growth, or return on investment.

If you put $10 into something and it becomes $20, your reward is the extra $10. If you run a lemonade stand, spend $30 on supplies, and bring in $100 over a weekend, your reward is the $70 profit—plus the experience and confidence gained along the way.

Rewards aren't always measured strictly in dollars. They can take the form of knowledge, business connections, or stronger opportunities next time. Still, in investing, reward is most often tied to how much your money grows and how quickly.

The Rule of the See-Saw

Picture a see-saw. On one side sits Risk. On the other sits Reward. When one rises, the other usually rises too. High risk often brings the possibility of high reward; low risk usually produces lower returns.

Low Risk, Low Reward:

- Savings accounts
- Government bonds

- Certificates of deposit (CDs)

These are safe and nearly guaranteed. But they grow slowly. For example, $100 in a savings account at 1% interest will only grow by $1 in a year.

Medium Risk, Medium Reward:

- Index funds
- Stocks from large, established companies
- Rental properties in stable neighborhoods

These can provide steady growth with some volatility. A stock might dip temporarily, or a rental unit could sit vacant for a month, but with patience and research the risks are manageable.

High Risk, High Reward:

- Startups or new businesses
- Penny stocks
- Cryptocurrency

These can create rapid wealth—or wipe it out just as quickly. Without research, strategy, and discipline, this type of risk becomes dangerous.

How to Manage Risk

Rich Dad often said: *"The biggest risk in life is not taking any."* But he wasn't encouraging reckless gambling. He meant you must learn the rules, then take informed risks.

Ways to manage risk wisely:

1. Educate Yourself – Knowledge reduces risk. Study the business model. Research the stock. Learn from people who've already done it.
2. Don't Invest What You Can't Lose – Never risk your emergency fund. Only use money you can set aside for the long term.
3. Diversify – Spread investments across different assets. If one fails, others can balance it out.
4. Start Small, Then Scale – Begin with modest investments. Learn lessons at a low cost before committing more.
5. Use Stop-Loss Strategies – Predetermine the maximum loss you'll accept. For example, if a stock drops 10%, you sell to prevent deeper losses.

Real-Life Story from *Rich Dad Poor Dad*

Robert Kiyosaki shared how his rich dad once bought a plain, unimpressive house near a school. Friends mocked him for choosing something "boring." But the property rented quickly to a teacher, producing reliable monthly cash flow.

The lesson: investments don't have to look glamorous to be profitable. The real risk lies in ignoring solid, predictable opportunities just because they don't seem exciting.

Why Most People Avoid Risk—And Why You Shouldn't

Many people remain financially stuck because they avoid risk altogether. They keep money in savings accounts, never invest, never start businesses.

Kiyosaki wrote: *"Most people never get rich because they are more afraid of losing than they are excited about winning."*

If fear outweighs excitement, opportunities slip away. Successful investors don't eliminate fear; they prepare for it and move forward anyway.

The Risk of Doing Nothing

Doing nothing carries its own risks:

1. Money sitting idle loses value over time due to inflation. $100 today won't buy the same in ten years.
2. Failing to grow wealth leaves you falling behind while others move ahead.

Risk doesn't only come from making bad moves—it also comes from standing still.

Learning to Love Calculated Risk

The path forward is not blind leaps but calculated risks. That means planning, preparing, and acting with purpose.

By now, you know the basics: assets versus liabilities, the role of cash flow. Use that knowledge to ask sharper questions before investing:

- Will this put money in my pocket or take it out?
- How risky is this compared to alternatives?
- What's the worst-case scenario?
- What's the best possible outcome?
- How can I protect myself if things go wrong?

Asking these questions turns risk into strategy, not guesswork.

Making Your Own Risk Ladder

A useful tool is creating a personal "risk ladder." List financial moves from least risky to most risky, then decide where you're comfortable starting. For example:

1. Keeping cash in a bank account
2. Buying a government bond
3. Investing in an index fund
4. Purchasing a single stock
5. Funding a friend's startup

Over time, as knowledge and confidence grow, you can climb higher on the ladder.

Risk Is a Muscle

Risk tolerance strengthens with practice. The first leap feels terrifying. The second, less so. By the third, you begin to feel confident.

Risk isn't about being fearless. It's about moving forward even with nerves in play. That's what separates successful investors, entrepreneurs, and creators from those who remain stuck.

Final Thought

You can't win the game of money by hiding on the sidelines. But you also shouldn't charge in blind.

The key lies in understanding risk, preparing carefully, and taking deliberate action. When you learn to work with risk instead of against it, you position yourself to grow.

Now that you've explored the balance of risk and reward, the next step is discovering how risk can fuel one of the greatest wealth-building strategies: starting your own business.

Key Points Recap

- Greater reward usually comes with greater risk.
- Always research before investing.
- Safe investments grow slowly but steadily.
- Risky investments can skyrocket or collapse quickly.
- Example: A new app can either flop or fly.
- Visual: A see-saw chart showing Risk on one side and Reward on the other.

Chapter 13:
Start Your Own Business

What if you could make your own money, solve a real problem, and be your own boss? Sounds exciting, right? Starting a business isn't just for adults in suits or people with offices downtown. The truth is—you don't need a shiny skyscraper, a stack of cash, or a fancy logo to begin. You just need three things: an idea, a plan, and the courage to take the first step.

When you start a business, something amazing happens. You stop waiting for others to hand you money—whether it's from allowance, gifts, or even a future paycheck. Instead, you start creating money for yourself. You shift from asking "Can I have some?" to declaring, "I made this."

And here's a secret: some of the world's most successful entrepreneurs started young—sometimes as kids just like you. Business isn't just about making money; it's about building freedom, learning life skills, and discovering lessons that school doesn't always cover.

So, let's dive into the exciting world of kid entrepreneurship.

The World Pays You to Solve Problems

Every single business exists for one reason: to solve a problem. That's it. If you can solve a problem faster, better, cheaper, or in a way that makes people happy, then congratulations—you're already thinking like a business owner.

Think about it for a moment.

- Why do people pay for lemonade? Because they're thirsty and want something cold and refreshing.
- Why do people buy video games? Because they're bored and want to be entertained.
- Why do parents hire someone to mow the lawn? Because they're busy and want the job done without having to spend their Saturday sweating under the sun.

Now ask yourself: *What problems do I see around me? What's missing here? What would make life easier, better, or more fun?*

That question—"What's missing?"—is the seed of every business idea. And the amazing thing is, kids often see problems that adults overlook.

For example, maybe your school's snack options are boring. Maybe the kids in your neighborhood don't have a fun activity after school. Maybe your friend struggles to set up a new video game console. Each of these is a small problem that could become the start of a small business.

Your First Business Doesn't Have to Be Big

A lot of people believe that to start a business, you need to invent something brand new, like the next iPhone, or launch a billion-dollar company. That's just not true. In fact, some of the best first businesses are simple, small, and local.

You could:

- Sell cold drinks at a soccer game.
- Walk dogs for neighbors who work late.
- Help grandparents set up their smartphones.
- Make art and sell it online.

- Tutor younger kids in math or reading.
- Build custom Minecraft worlds and charge for access.

Here's the key: start with what you enjoy and look for what others need.

Take this story as an example: Maya, a 10-year-old, loved making slime. She noticed her friends wanted glittery, colorful slime but couldn't find it in stores. So, Maya started customizing slime and selling it in her neighborhood. Within two months, she made over $600—just by turning her hobby into a business.

Maya didn't wait for someone to hire her. She created value—and got paid.

What Does a Business Actually Do?

Let's break it down into six simple steps. Every business has:

1. The Problem – What issue are you solving?
2. The Product or Service – What are you offering that solves it?
3. The Customer – Who needs this, and why?
4. The Price – How much will you charge, and how much does it cost you to make or provide?
5. The Profit – What's left after subtracting your costs from your price.
6. The Plan – How will you let people know and deliver what they buy?

If you can answer those six questions, congratulations— you already understand more about business than many adults.

You Inc. Levels Up

Earlier, we talked about how you are the CEO of You Inc. That means you manage your time, energy, and money like a business.

When you start a real business, you take that concept to the next level. Now you're not just managing your personal finances—you're creating a system that brings in money, sometimes even when you're not directly working.

That's what entrepreneurs do. They build systems. A lemonade stand is a simple system. A kid who rents out soccer cleats at practice is building a system. Each step you take builds a little machine that makes money, teaches you skills, and grows over time.

Robert Kiyosaki puts it this way: *"The rich focus on building systems that generate cash flow."* That's your goal—even in a small business.

The Entrepreneur's Mindset

Let's be real: starting a business is exciting, but it's not always easy.

- Some ideas won't work.
- Some customers will say "no thanks."
- Some days, it'll feel like nothing is going right.

And that's okay.

Being an entrepreneur doesn't mean avoiding problems. It means solving them. Every challenge teaches you something new. Every mistake is a lesson in disguise.

Instead of getting discouraged, get curious.

Ask yourself: *Why didn't this work? What can I change? Who can I learn from?*

That's exactly how successful entrepreneurs think.

Story Time: Jordan and the Energy Bar

Jordan, age 12, loved basketball. After practice one day, he realized the vending machine only had candy and soda—nothing healthy. So, he experimented at home and made no-bake energy bars with oats, honey, and peanut butter.

He brought a few to practice and gave them out for free. The next day, kids were asking for more. Jordan started charging a dollar per bar. By the end of the week, he'd made $20. The next month, he was making $100.

Jordan learned how to keep track of ingredients, test recipes, and even design labels. His idea grew from a simple snack into a real business.

What started as one small problem—no healthy snacks—became the foundation for something bigger.

Start Small, Think Big

When you're just starting out, don't worry about making a million dollars. Focus on learning, creating value, and growing step by step.

If you can earn your first $10, you can earn $100. If you can earn $100, you can earn $1,000.

Business is a ladder you climb one rung at a time. Most adult entrepreneurs wish they'd started earlier. You're already ahead of the game.

Along the way, you'll also learn real-world skills:

- Talking to customers
- Budgeting
- Managing time
- Problem solving
- Marketing

These are the exact same skills CEOs, investors, and business owners use every single day.

Know Your Numbers

Every smart business owner knows their numbers.

Here are the three basics:

- Cost – How much does it cost to make your product or deliver your service?
- Price – How much are you charging people?
- Profit – What's left after subtracting your costs from your price.

Let's say you're selling bracelets. The beads, string, and packaging cost you $1.50 per bracelet. You sell each one for $5. That means your profit is $3.50.

- Sell 10 bracelets = $35 profit
- Sell 100 bracelets = $350 profit

But what if no one buys them? That's where numbers help you adjust. Maybe your price is too high. Maybe your designs need work. Numbers help you make better decisions instead of just guessing.

Marketing: Let People Know

Here's a truth many beginners forget: even the best product in the world won't sell if nobody knows about it. That's where marketing comes in.

Marketing is just telling the right people about your solution in a way that makes them want to buy.

For young entrepreneurs, marketing can be as simple as:

1. Talking to classmates or parents' friends.
2. Handing out flyers or posters.
3. Sharing on social media (with a parent's help).
4. Asking for referrals—"If you liked this, could you tell a friend?"
5. Relying on word-of-mouth—happy customers are the best salespeople.

Build Once, Earn Often

One of the most powerful ideas in business is this: build something once, earn from it many times.

Think about it:

- Write an eBook and sell it over and over.
- Design a sticker and sell it online.
- Create a dog-walking schedule and get paid every week.

Compare that to a job where you work one hour and get paid once. A business multiplies your time and effort.

Types of Kid Businesses

Here are a few categories to inspire you:

1. Digital businesses – eBooks, coding projects, YouTube channels, graphic design.
2. Service businesses – tutoring, pet care, tech help, babysitting, lawn care.
3. Product businesses – crafts, snacks, T-shirts, bracelets.
4. Creative businesses – music lessons, art commissions, storytelling.
5. Subscription businesses – monthly snack boxes, mystery packs, mini magazines.

Some of these might stay small and fun. Others could grow into something much bigger. Some kid entrepreneurs build real companies by the time they're in high school. Even if you don't, the skills you gain will last forever.

Be Legal, Be Safe

Before launching any business, talk to your parents or a trusted adult. Some businesses have rules—especially if you're selling food, using apps, or collecting payments. Adults can help you handle the official side of things.

And always, always stay safe. If you're meeting customers, make sure your parents know where you are. Don't share private details online. Protect your reputation, because your name is your most valuable brand.

Your Business is a Mini-Asset

Remember when we talked about assets—the things that put money in your pocket? A business is one of the best assets you can create.

A business earns money.
It can grow in value.
It can even be sold one day.

But more importantly, a business grows *you*. It builds your confidence, independence, and future.

Robert Kiyosaki often says: *"Your business is your greatest asset. Build it wisely."*

So what are you waiting for? Start something today. Test it. Improve it. Grow it.

Your first dollar earned from your own idea is worth more than any allowance.

Key Points

- Every business solves a problem.
- Kids can start simple businesses using skills or hobbies.
- Running a business teaches responsibility and creativity.
- Know your numbers: cost, price, profit.
- Reinvest profits to grow.
- Example: selling healthy snacks at school.
- Visual: "Kid Entrepreneur Kit" showing idea, plan, customers, and money flow.

Chapter 14:
Compound Growth — Your Money's Superpower

Imagine you planted a single apple seed in your backyard. At first, nothing much happens. You water it, maybe even forget it's there. Days pass, then weeks. Eventually, a tiny sprout appears. That sprout becomes a sapling. Years later, you have a full-grown tree producing dozens of apples. And here's the kicker: every apple carries more seeds, and those seeds can grow into more trees.

That's exactly how compound growth works.

It doesn't look like much in the beginning. But with time, consistency, and patience, the effect multiplies, turning small efforts into large results.

Most people — especially kids, but even plenty of adults — think the only path to "more money" is to *earn* it: mowing lawns, babysitting, getting a job, or selling something. But what if money itself could work for you, even while you're asleep?

That's the hidden magic of compound growth.

What Is Compound Growth?

At its core, compound growth is when your money earns returns — and then those returns earn returns of their own.

Think of it this way: it's not just linear growth (one step forward each time). It's exponential growth — growth stacked on top of growth.

Here's a simple demonstration:

- Year 1: You save $100 in an account that pays 10% yearly interest. At the end of the year, you earn $10, leaving you with $110.
- Year 2: Now your $110 earns 10%. That's $11. New total: $121.
- Year 3: 10% of $121 is $12.10. New total: $133.10.
- Year 4: 10% of $133.10 is $13.31. New total: $146.41.

Notice how the earnings increase each year — even though you never added another dollar. That's because your interest is compounding: interest on interest, returns on returns.

This is why Albert Einstein supposedly called compound growth the "eighth wonder of the world."

The Snowball Story

Imagine rolling a small snowball down a hill. At first, it barely changes. But as it continues rolling, it gathers more snow. With each turn, it grows faster and bigger. Eventually, the tiny snowball is massive — almost unstoppable.

Compound growth behaves exactly the same way. It feels slow in the early stages, but the longer you let it roll, the more momentum it gains.

The Rule of 72

Want a quick way to predict how long it will take your money to double? Use the Rule of 72.

Divide 72 by the annual rate of return. The result is the approximate number of years it takes to double your money.

- At 6% growth per year: $72 \div 6 = 12$ years to double.
- At 9% growth per year: $72 \div 9 = 8$ years to double.

So, if you invest $100 at 9% interest, you'd have:

- $200 in 8 years
- $400 in 16 years
- $800 in 24 years
- $1,600 in 32 years

All without adding another cent. That's compounding at work.

How the Rich Use Compound Growth

Robert Kiyosaki, author of *Rich Dad Poor Dad*, explains: *"The rich don't work for money. They make money work for them."*

The wealthy understand compounding. They invest in assets like stocks, rental properties, or businesses that generate steady returns. And instead of spending those returns, they reinvest them — creating layer after layer of compounding.

- "Poor Dad" might say: *"Work hard, save a little."*
- "Rich Dad" might say: *"Make your money work harder than you do."*

It's less about working nonstop, and more about positioning your time and money to create repeating, multiplying returns.

Simple vs. Compound Interest

To see why compounding is so powerful, compare it with simple interest.

- With simple interest, $100 at 10% per year earns $10 each year, forever. After five years, you'd have $150.
- With compound interest, $100 at 10% grows like this: $110 → $121 → $133.10 → $146.41 → $161.05.

That's $11.05 more in just five years. Over decades, that "extra bit" snowballs into thousands.

The Superpower of Starting Early

Here's the real secret: time is the biggest multiplier in compounding.

Consider two kids:

- Kid A saves $1,000 each year from age 10 to 20 — then stops forever.
- Kid B saves $1,000 each year from age 20 to 60.

By age 60, Kid A (who saved only 10 years' worth) actually ends up with more money than Kid B. Why? Because Kid A's money had decades of extra time to compound.

This is why financial educators say: *"Time in the market beats timing the market."*

Compound Growth Beyond Money

Compounding isn't just financial. It happens in life too.

- Knowledge compounds: Reading 10 pages daily adds up to entire libraries over a lifetime.
- Skills compound: Practicing an instrument or a sport daily makes you exponentially better over years.
- Habits compound: Eating one apple won't make you healthy. Eating one daily for a year transforms your body.

Small, consistent actions stack to create massive outcomes.

What Grows Fast vs. Slow

Not every form of compounding grows at the same pace.

- Savings accounts: Typically under 1% per year — very slow growth.
- Stocks/index funds: Historically 7–10% per year, though with more risk.
- Real estate: Can grow through both rental income and property value appreciation.
- Businesses: Reinvesting profits can create rapid compound growth if the business scales.

The rule of thumb: higher potential growth usually comes with higher risk.

Doubling with Compounding

Let's imagine you invest $1,000 and it doubles every 6 years:

- Year 0: $1,000
- Year 6: $2,000
- Year 12: $4,000
- Year 18: $8,000
- Year 24: $16,000
- Year 30: $32,000
- Year 36: $64,000
- Year 42: $128,000

That's the power of doubling. You didn't work extra. You didn't save more. Time and compounding did the heavy lifting.

What If You Wait Too Long?

Consider Jasmine and Jake:

- Jasmine invests $2,000 yearly from ages 12 to 22, then stops.
- Jake starts at age 30 and invests $2,000 yearly until 60.

Jake invests much more overall, but Jasmine ends up ahead because her money had extra years to compound.

In compounding, *time matters more than amount.*

Common Mistakes to Avoid

1. Spending your interest instead of reinvesting it.

2. Waiting too long to start. Delay reduces compounding power.
3. Stopping halfway. Compounding only works if you're consistent.
4. Parking money in ultra-low-interest accounts forever.

Practical Ways to Harness Compounding

- Open a high-interest savings or investment account.
- Use stocks or index funds with automatic reinvestment.
- Start a small business or side hustle and reinvest profits.
- Invest in your own learning and skills — the highest long-term return.
- Track progress with charts or apps to "see" compounding in action.

Mini-Story: The Tree and the Candy

Liam got $100 for his birthday. His first thought? Candy. But his older cousin explained investing.

Instead of spending, Liam used a kid-friendly investing app. Each year, the money grew: $100 → $110 → $121 → $133.

Three years later, Liam had enough to buy candy *and* a bike. Better yet, his money was still growing.

That's the difference between consuming and compounding.

Be Patient — Compounding Is Slow at First

At the start, growth feels invisible. But given enough time, the curve bends upward, becoming almost explosive.

Most of the magic happens toward the end — which is why consistency and early action are everything.

Your Compound Growth Challenge

Pick one habit today — saving $10 a week, reading 20 minutes daily, or reinvesting part of your allowance. Track it for one year.

You'll see how small actions, multiplied by time, create results that feel almost magical.

Key Points Recap:

- Compound growth = earning interest on your interest.
- Time + consistency are the real superpowers.
- Starting young gives a huge advantage.
- Compounding applies to money, knowledge, skills, and habits.
- Example: $100 invested with time can grow into thousands.

Your Money Playbook: One Last Pass

Money follows value. That has been the thread through every chapter, and it is the thread you can keep pulling for the rest of your life. You do not need perfect timing or perfect tools. You need a real problem, a useful response, and the habit of measuring what happens so you can do it a little better next time. The pages behind you were meant to turn money from a mystery into a set of simple moves you can practice.

Chapter 1

You learned the language of money so you can think clearly and act clearly. Income, expenses, assets, liabilities, and cash flow are not big words. They are labels that help you see what is real. When you can name what is happening, you can change what is happening.

Chapter 2

You started with action. Earning came first because earning teaches faster than reading about earning. Small services, tiny products, and simple useful help are training for bigger things. Value first, money next.

Chapter 3

You slowed down your spending long enough to choose it. Tracking showed where money actually goes. With that picture in front of you, wants and needs stop blurring together. Control shows up when attention shows up.

Chapter 4

You wrote a balance sheet and saw your true score. Assets on one side, liabilities on the other, and the difference in the middle. Looking at that page every month turns guesses into a plan.

Chapter 5

You built an income and expense statement so "where did it all go" stopped being a monthly surprise. Listing what comes in and what goes out makes waste obvious and priorities honest. That is how profit begins at home.

Chapter 6

You watched cash flow, which is money in motion. It told you whether your life is funding your goals or draining them. When the flow is positive, you have options. When it is not, you have a clear place to work.

Chapter 7

You drew a line between assets and liabilities. Assets put money in your pocket. Liabilities take money out. Owning more assets, and using liabilities with care, is how freedom grows.

Chapter 8

You picked one goal that matters and gave it a number and a date. A simple plan plus steady effort beats complicated ideas that never leave the page. Progress you can see keeps you going.

Chapter 9

You ran You Inc. like a small, focused business. Time, energy, and dollars got a job description. Systems replaced willpower. Routines did the heavy lifting so results showed up even on ordinary days.

Chapter 10

You met stocks as slices of real businesses. Prices move with performance and emotion, so patience matters. Buying well and holding long lets other people's hard work pay you over time.

Chapter 11

You met real estate as land and buildings that can pay rent and grow in value. Managed with care, property becomes an asset that works while you work on other things. The key is numbers first, excitement second.

Chapter 12

You faced risk without fear. Risk and reward travel together, so you sized your bets, protected the downside, and took only the risks you could understand. Courage plus common sense is a strong pair.

Chapter 13

You started a small business on purpose. Find a person, solve a problem, price for profit, and keep your promise. Reinvest early wins into better tools, better skills, and better service. That is how tiny becomes steady.

Chapter 14

You gave your money time to compound. Returns that earn returns can look slow at first, then surprising later. Starting now matters more than starting big. Consistency is the secret you can control.

Last Word

If there is one direction to carry out of this book, it is simple: create value, track the numbers, buy or build assets, and give your choices enough time to work. Pick one useful action you can take in the next day, then another next week, then another next month. Money will follow the value you keep creating.

www.ingramcontent.com/pod-product-compliance
Lightning Source LLC
Chambersburg PA
CBHW071202300726
48975CB00004B/1253